Dear Child,

Can you imagine if someone said that people with big noses were better than people with small noses? Wouldn't that be silly? Well, when I was growing up in South Africa, we were told something just as strange. We were told that people with darker skin were not quite as wonderful as people with lighter skin. Can you imagine? But that's the way it was for a long time, and many mean things were said and done during those bad old days.

You are about to read a story about a young boy named Desmond who looks a lot like me – although he doesn't have all this funny grey hair. In this story, Desmond learns the power of words and the secret of forgiveness.

Desmond Tutu

Desmond
and the
Very Mean Word

A STORY OF FORGIVENESS

Archbishop Desmond Tutu
and Douglas Carlton Abrams

illustrated by A. G. Ford

WALKER BOOKS
AND SUBSIDIARIES

LONDON • BOSTON • SYDNEY • AUCKLAND

DESMOND WAS VERY PROUD of his new bicycle. He was the only child in the whole township who had one, and he couldn't wait to show it to Father Trevor.

Father Trevor was kind and loving, and when he laughed, his eyes sparkled and his whole body shook. Father Trevor didn't care if you were rich or poor, black or white, old or young. He raised his hat and smiled at everyone he met. He especially loved the children and would even let them play marbles on the floor of his office, where he met the many important people who came to visit.

As Desmond sped down the dirt road, he admired the bicycle's shiny black body and the white stripe on the rear mudguard. Oh, it was beautiful!

When he turned the corner, he saw a gang of boys – and they saw him. They stepped into the road and blocked his path. He didn't dare stop. What if they took his bike? Desmond gripped the handlebar and raced toward the boys, dust flying behind him.

The boys scattered out of the way, but the tallest, a red-haired boy, spat out a very mean word. The other boys laughed and shouted the mean word again and again. Desmond pedalled away as fast as he could. His heart pounded and his chest ached.

When Desmond got to Father Trevor's office, he threw down his bicycle. His teeth were clenched, and the mean word kept repeating itself over and over inside his head like an echo in a dark cave.

Father Trevor looked up as Desmond burst into his office. "What's wrong?" he asked, excusing himself from a meeting. Father Trevor always knew when something was wrong.

"Nothing," Desmond said.

Father Trevor bent down until he was looking directly into Desmond's face. His smiling eyes always made you feel you were the most important person in the world. "You can tell me anything."

Desmond glanced down at his dusty bare feet and finally muttered, "Some boys … they shouted a very mean word at me."

"I'm sorry that happened," Father Trevor said. "They hurt your feelings, didn't they."

Desmond's shoulders relaxed a little, and he nodded.

"Can you forgive them?" Father Trevor asked.

"No! Never!" Desmond said, his fists balled at his sides. "I will get them back!"

Father Trevor sighed. "That is the problem, Desmond. You will get them back, and then they will get you back, and soon our whole world will be filled with nothing but 'getting back'."

THAT NIGHT, Desmond lay in bed, trying to read his comic book by candlelight. Instead of the words on the page, he kept seeing the mean word written over and over again.

THE NEXT DAY, no matter how fast he pedalled to school, Desmond couldn't leave the mean word behind. All day the mean word followed him around like a shadow in the hot sun.

As he rode home that afternoon, he saw the boys again. His hands and face felt hot. Maybe, he thought, if he got even, he would stop thinking about what they had called him. So he raced past the boys and shouted the meanest word he could think of. He could hear the boys running after him. Desmond pedalled hard, his heart pounding. Finally, he looked back: the boys had given up the chase.

At first Desmond felt proud, but very soon he began to feel something else. It was not a good feeling. The mean word he had said left a bitter taste in his mouth.

AFTER SCHOOL the next day, Desmond went to Father Trevor's.

"Are you feeling any better, Desmond?" Father Trevor asked, as he sat on the floor playing marbles with the children.

Desmond shook his head from side to side and frowned.

"When people say mean words to us, we often feel ashamed of who we are," Father Trevor said. "They can make us feel a little less lovable, but we aren't." Lowering his face close to the floor, Father Trevor lined up one of the smaller marbles in the chalk circle. "Desmond, everything we do matters – if we smile or if we frown, if we say something nice or something mean." Father Trevor flicked the big marble with his thumb and hit the smaller marble out of the circle.

"When we hurt someone," Father Trevor said as he got up, "it hurts us, too."

THAT NIGHT, Father Trevor dropped in to see Desmond's parents. Desmond carried a pot of tea into the living room and then went outside. Usually he would try to listen to what the adults were saying, but that night he just wanted to be alone. Sitting on the doorstep, Desmond looked up at the starry sky, an empty ache in his chest. He thought he could even see the mean word written on the face of the moon.

"That's a very nice bicycle you have," Father Trevor said as he sat down next to Desmond. The black paint gleamed in the moonlight.

Desmond had forgotten to show his bike to Father Trevor. It didn't matter now. He just shrugged and turned his back. He didn't want to talk, not even to Father Trevor.

"Still thinking about that mean word?" Father Trevor asked.

Desmond slowly nodded.

"Our hearts are fragile and easily hurt. This is why we were given a way to heal them – it's called forgiveness."

"How can I forgive them? They haven't said they're sorry."

"You don't need to wait until someone says they're sorry to forgive them. You have the power to forgive whenever you are ready."

"I'm not ready," Desmond said.

"That's fine, Desmond. Only you will know when you are." Father Trevor got up to leave.

Desmond felt a lump in his throat.

Father Trevor said very softly, "Let me tell you a secret, Desmond. When you forgive someone, you free yourself from what they have said or done. It's like magic."

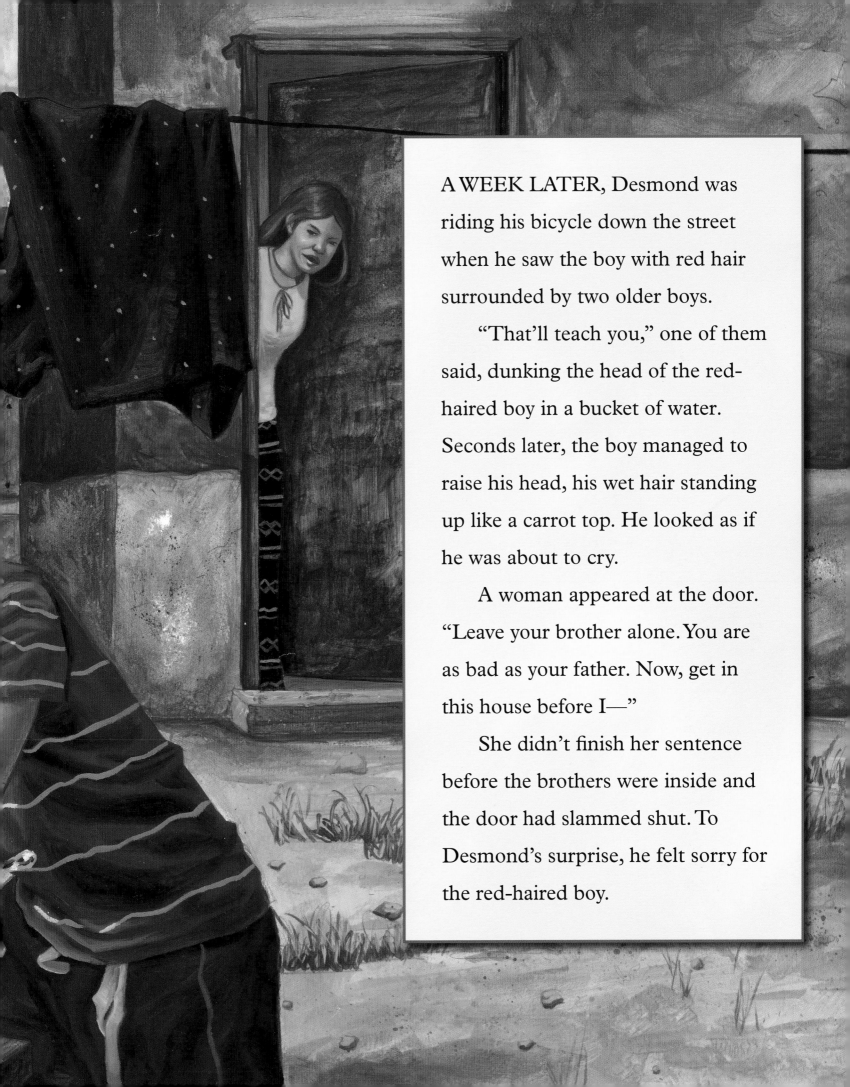

A WEEK LATER, Desmond was riding his bicycle down the street when he saw the boy with red hair surrounded by two older boys.

"That'll teach you," one of them said, dunking the head of the red-haired boy in a bucket of water. Seconds later, the boy managed to raise his head, his wet hair standing up like a carrot top. He looked as if he was about to cry.

A woman appeared at the door. "Leave your brother alone. You are as bad as your father. Now, get in this house before I—"

She didn't finish her sentence before the brothers were inside and the door had slammed shut. To Desmond's surprise, he felt sorry for the red-haired boy.

A FEW DAYS LATER, Desmond ran into the neighbourhood market to buy his father a newspaper. Out of the corner of his eye, he saw a flash of red. Turning, Desmond realized it was the red-haired boy. He was standing alone in front of the sweet counter. It was filled with lollipops and delicious-looking chocolates.

Desmond wanted to say something, but what?

Thinking of the mean word he had shouted at the boy, Desmond finally blurted out, "I'm sorry for what I said."

The boy looked at him, speechless. Finally he stammered, "I guess … I'm … well…"

Desmond didn't need the boy to say he was sorry. It would have been nice, but as Father Trevor had said, it really wasn't necessary.

"I forgive you," Desmond said quietly. As soon as the words were out of his mouth, Desmond felt a little stronger and a little braver and stood up a little taller.

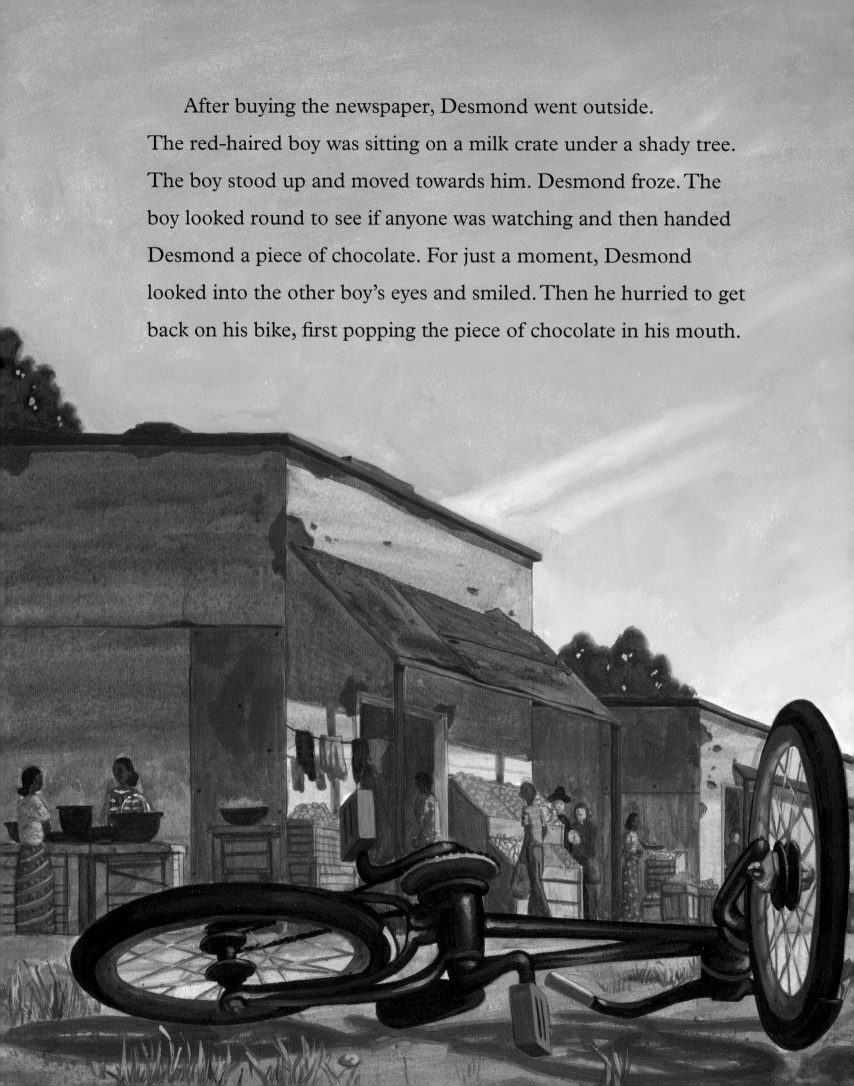

After buying the newspaper, Desmond went outside. The red-haired boy was sitting on a milk crate under a shady tree. The boy stood up and moved towards him. Desmond froze. The boy looked round to see if anyone was watching and then handed Desmond a piece of chocolate. For just a moment, Desmond looked into the other boy's eyes and smiled. Then he hurried to get back on his bike, first popping the piece of chocolate in his mouth.

As the sun set behind the houses, Desmond pedalled home fast, not out of fear but out of joy. The cool wind felt good against his face. He wanted the sweet taste of chocolate on his tongue to last for ever.

Slowly he spread his arms out wide as if he were flying. At last he knew what it felt like to be free. It was as if he could embrace the whole world in his outstretched arms.

AUTHOR'S NOTE

This story was inspired by something that actually happened to me when I was growing up in South Africa. Father Trevor is based on Father Trevor Huddleston, who was my childhood hero and really would let children play marbles in his office. Father Trevor mentored me and countless other young people. When I was ill in hospital for twenty months, he came to visit me – one poor boy in his whole parish – every single week. At another time, he asked Louis Armstrong for a trumpet, which he gave to a young boy named Hugh. Hugh Masekela became one of South Africa's greatest trumpeters. Father Trevor, who eventually became Archbishop Huddleston, was one of the most important members of the anti-apartheid movement – the name given to all those who worked together for an equal and just South Africa. He truly did care about everyone and in many different ways taught us the secrets of love and forgiveness. In his honour, my wife, Leah, and I named our first son Trevor.

This book is dedicated to Father Trevor Huddleston
who taught us to forgive and helped us to free South Africa.

It is also dedicated to our children and grandchildren
and to all people – young and old – who discover the freedom of forgiveness.
D. T. & D. C. A.

To my high-school art teacher, Jeff Steed
A. G. F.

First published 2013 by Walker Books Ltd
87 Vauxhall Walk, London SE11 5HJ

This edition published 2022

2 4 6 8 10 9 7 5 3 1

Text © 2013 Desmond M. Tutu
Illustrations © 2013 A. G. Ford

The right of Desmond M. Tutu and A. G. Ford to be identified as author and illustrator respectively of this work
has been asserted in accordance with the Copyright, Designs and Patents Act 1988

This book has been typeset in Plantin

Printed in Malta

British Library Cataloguing in Publication Data:
a catalogue record for this book is available from the British Library

ISBN 978-1-5295-1045-4

www.walker.co.uk